LITTLE
COPY CUB

Catherine & Laurence Anholt

PUFFIN BOOKS

In the big and busy jungle,

Little Cub is growing up.

He wants to
be *just* like
Big Golden Lion.

Little Cub copies Big Golden Lion.
Can you copy too?

"You are my Little Copy Cub," says Big Golden Lion. "And I am very proud of you."

Little Cub goes walking all by himself
in the big and busy jungle.

He doesn't know that Big Golden Lion
is watching from behind the trees.

Little Cub wants to copy all
the things his friends can do.

Little Cub meets
Tiny Mouse.

Tiny Mouse can twitch
her wispy whiskers and
squeak a tiny squeak …

"Sque-e-e-ak, sque-e-e-ak!"

Little Cub can
squeak too.
Can you?

"Sque-e-e-ak, sque-e-e-ak!"

Tiny Mouse can
roll up tight in a
funny, furry ball.

Little Cub can
roll up too.
Can you?

Tiny Mouse can
tickle and tumble
topsy-turvy.

Little Cub can
tickle too.
Can you?

Tiny Mouse can scurry and scamper
and scuttle down her tiny mousy hole.

But ... Little Cub *can't* copy that.
And neither can you!

So Little Cub walks further and further into the big and busy jungle. He wants to copy all the things his friends can do.

Little Cub meets Big Baby Hippo.

Big Baby Hippo can splash and splosh and make bubbly hippo noises …

"Blibble, blabble, blubble!"

Little Cub can bubble too. *Can you?*

"Blibble, blabble, blubble!"

Big Baby Hippo
can open his big,
wide mouth and
smile a *huge*
hippo smile.

Little Cub can
smile too.
Can you?

Big Baby Hippo
can do a wibbly
wobbly hippo
wiggle.

Little Cub can
wiggle too.
Can you?

Big Baby Hippo can dive
deep down into the cool
blue pool and squirt water
way up into the air.

But ... Little Cub *can't* copy that.
And neither can you!

So Little Cub walks even further into the big and busy jungle. He wants to copy all the things his friends can do.

Little Cub meets Gentle Giraffe.

Gentle Giraffe can swish her tail and crunch and munch her lunch …

"Munch, crunch, munch!"

Little Cub can munch too.
Can you?

"Munch, crunch, munch!"

Gentle Giraffe can
bend right down
to the ground and
touch her toes
with her nose.

Little Cub can
touch his toes too.
Can you?

Gentle Giraffe can dance and sway slowly
from side to side.

Little Cub
can dance
and sway too.
Can you?

Gentle Giraffe can stretch right up to the top of the very tallest tree.

But … Little Cub
can't copy that.
And neither can you!

So Little Cub walks even further still into the big and busy jungle. He wants to copy all the things his friends can do.

Little Cub meets Giggly Gorilla.

Giggly Gorilla can pat her chest and grunt a great gorilla grunt …

"UUHH-OOHH, UUHH-OOHH!"

Little Cub can grunt too. *Can you?*

"UUHH-OOHH, UUHH-OOHH!"

Giggly Gorilla
can jump and jig
and roll head
over heels.

Little Cub can
roll too.
Can you?

Giggly Gorilla can
rough and tumble
and give a great
gorilla hug.

Little Cub can
hug too.
Can you?

Giggly Gorilla can charge
through the jungle and

s-w-i-n-g

from tree to tree.

But … Little Cub *can't* copy that.
And neither can you!

As night time falls, Little Cub walks right into the deep, dark middle of the big and busy jungle. He still wants to copy all the things his friends can do.

Little Cub meets Round Brown Owl.

Round Brown Owl can go out in the dark without ever being afraid and … ho-oo-t …

"Tu-whit tu-whoo-oo!"

Little Cub can hoot, tu-whit tu-whoo too. *Can yoo-ou?*

"Tu-whit tu-whoo-oo!"

Round Brown Owl
can spread her wide
and wonderful
wings and hop up
on to a higher
branch.

Little Cub can (just about) hop too.
Can you?

Round Brown Owl
can swoop into the
sky and fly far away,
up above the
moonlit jungle.

But …

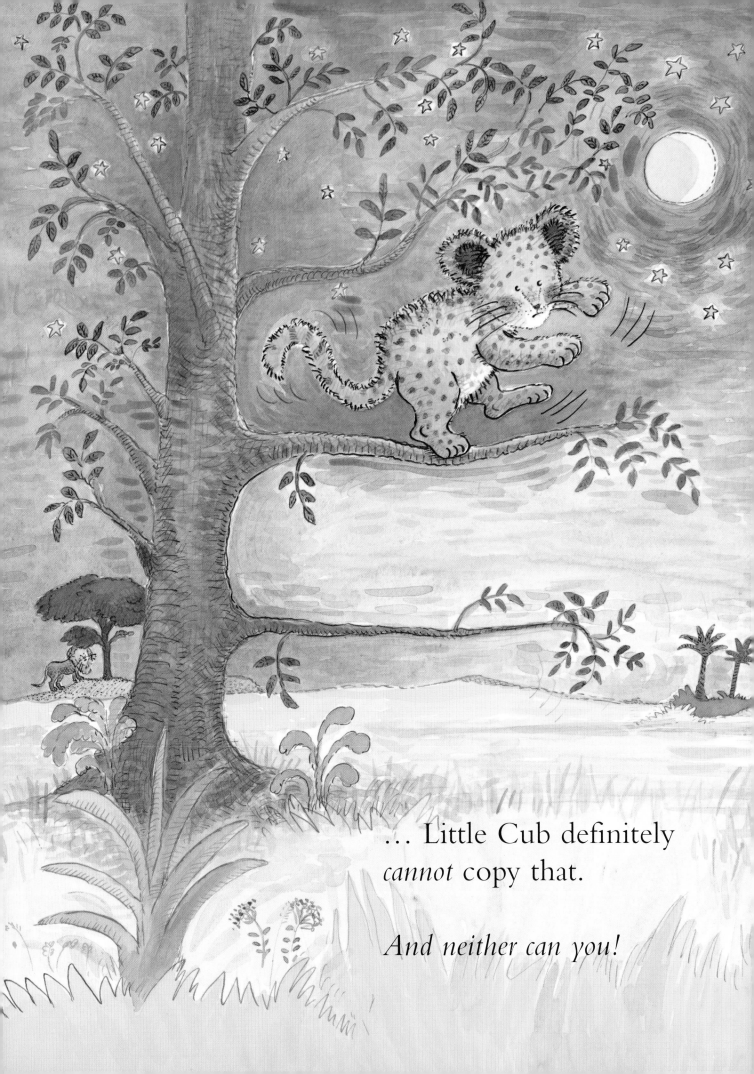

... Little Cub definitely *cannot* copy that.

And neither can you!

Little Cub falls
down,

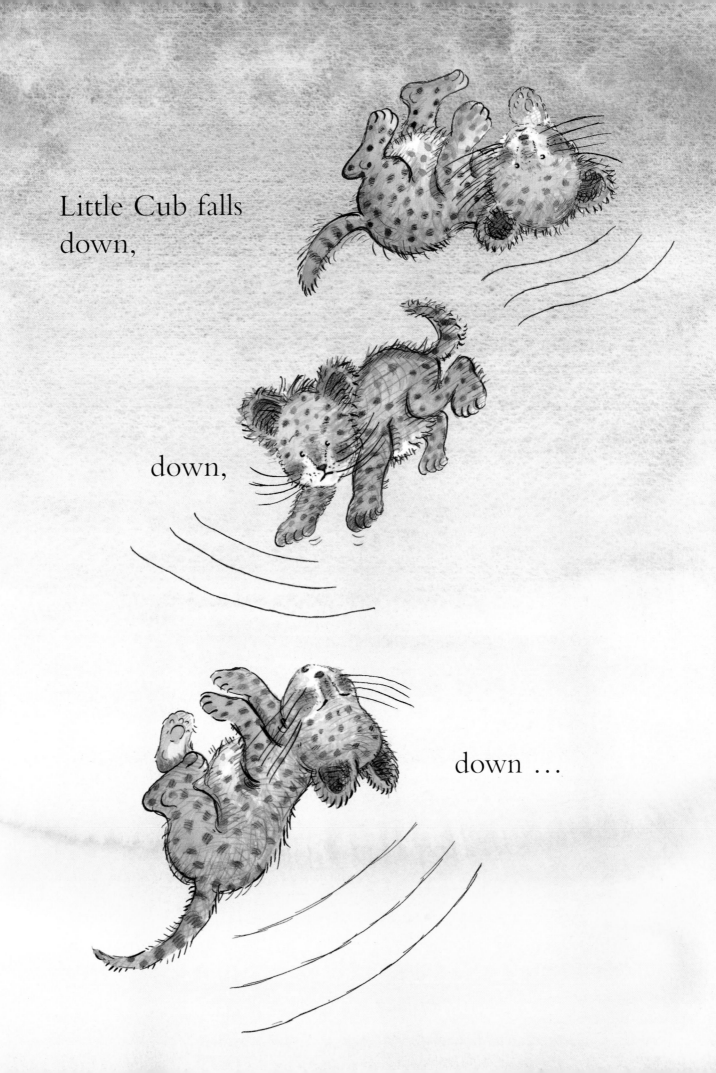

down,

down …

… right into the safe, strong paws of Big Golden Lion.

"Listen, Little Copy Cub," says Big Golden Lion. "You are getting big and brave. But you are still my little cub and you need to take care in the big and busy jungle."

Lions must do what lions do best.

Like sneaking home through the silent shadows without a single sound.

Cubs can do that too.

Like str-e-e-tching and curling up close and yawning Golden Lion yawns …

"Yaraawwaal!"

Cubs can do that too.

"Yaraawwaal!"

Like falling asleep under shiny stars and
dreaming Golden Lion dreams…

"Shh!"

Cubs can do that too.

"Shhhhhhhhh!"

Little Copy Cub is sleeping now.

But one day he will be BIG and BRAVE and GROWN UP too.

And so will you.

For

Sam and Hannah White

PUFFIN BOOKS

Published by the Penguin Group
Penguin Books Ltd, 27 Wrights Lane, London W8 5TZ, England
Penguin Putnam Inc., 375 Hudson Street, New York, New York 10014, USA
Penguin Books Australia Ltd, Ringwood, Victoria, Australia
Penguin Books Canada Ltd, 10 Alcorn Avenue, Toronto, Ontario, Canada M4V 3B2
Penguin Books (NZ) Ltd, Private Bag 102902, NSMC, Auckland, New Zealand

Penguin Books Ltd, Registered Offices: Harmondsworth, Middlesex, England

On the World Wide Web at: www.penguin.com

First published by Hamish Hamilton Ltd 1999
Published in Puffin Books 2000
1 3 5 7 9 10 8 6 4 2

Text copyright © Laurence Anholt, 1999
Illustrations copyright © Catherine Anholt, 1999
All rights reserved

The moral right of the author and illustrator has been asserted

Made and printed in Italy by Printer Trento Srl

British Library Cataloguing in Publication Data
A CIP catalogue record for this book is available from the British Library

ISBN 0–140–56423–3